# THERE WAS AN OLD LADY WHO SWALLOWED A GHOST!

by Lucille Colandro
Illustrated by Jared Lee

Cartwheel Books
an imprint of Scholastic Inc.

For Shelly and Kate who work to make books a treat for all.
— L.C.

To Charles D. Horsley, M.D.
— J.L.

ISBN 978-1-338-66829-2

10 9 8 7 6 5 4 3 2                                                         20 21 22 23 24

Printed in the U.S.A.     40
First printing 2020

There was an old lady who swallowed a ghost.
I don't know why she swallowed a ghost.
But she didn't boast.

There was an old lady who swallowed a mask.
Nobody had to ask why she swallowed that mask.

She swallowed the mask to hide the ghost.
I don't know why she swallowed a ghost.
But she didn't boast.

There was an old lady
who swallowed a spider.
Her mouth opened wider
to fit in the spider.

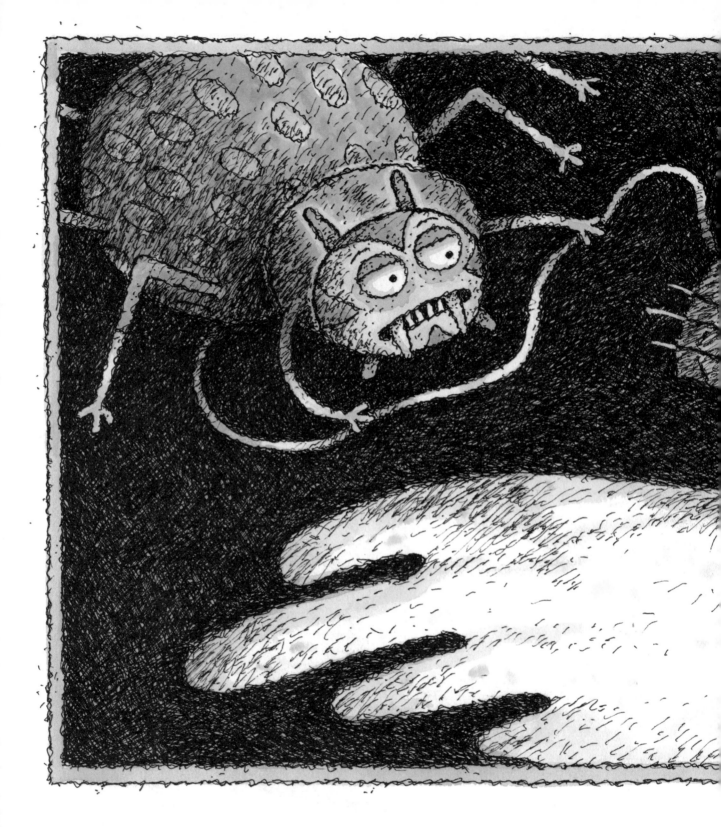

She swallowed the spider to string up the mask.
She swallowed the mask to hide the ghost.

I don't know why she swallowed a ghost.
But she didn't boast.

There was an old lady who swallowed a flashlight.

It made a splash right when she
swallowed the flashlight.

She swallowed the flashlight to brighten the spider.
She swallowed the spider to string up the mask.
She swallowed the mask to hide the ghost.

I don't know why she swallowed a ghost.
But she didn't boast.

There was an old lady who swallowed a cloak.
She didn't choke when she swallowed that cloak.

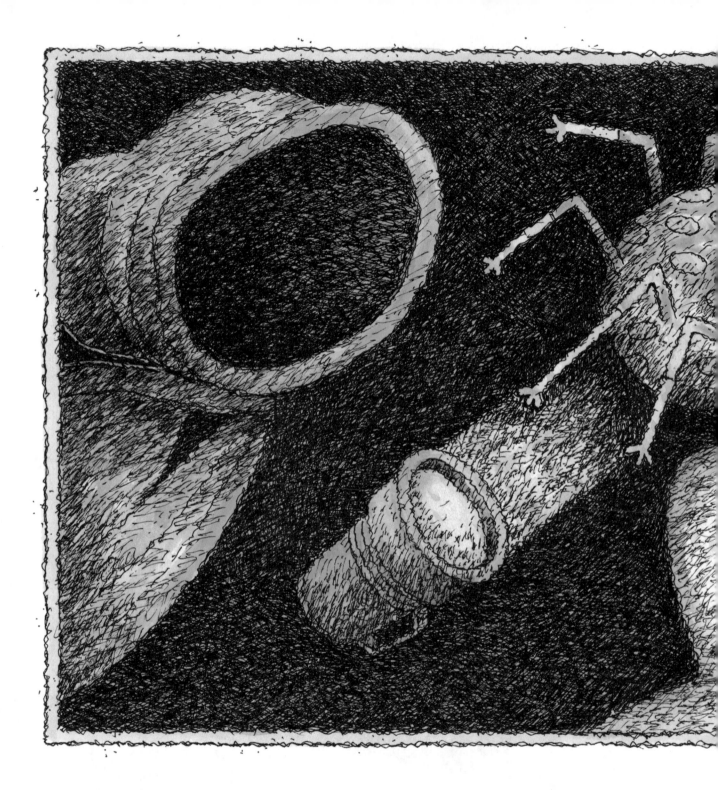

She swallowed the cloak to cover the flashlight.
She swallowed the flashlight to brighten the spider.
She swallowed the spider to string up the mask.

She swallowed the mask to hide the ghost.
I don't know why she swallowed a ghost.
But she didn't boast.

There was an old lady who swallowed some crows.

Everybody knows why she swallowed those crows.

She swallowed the crows to lift the cloak.

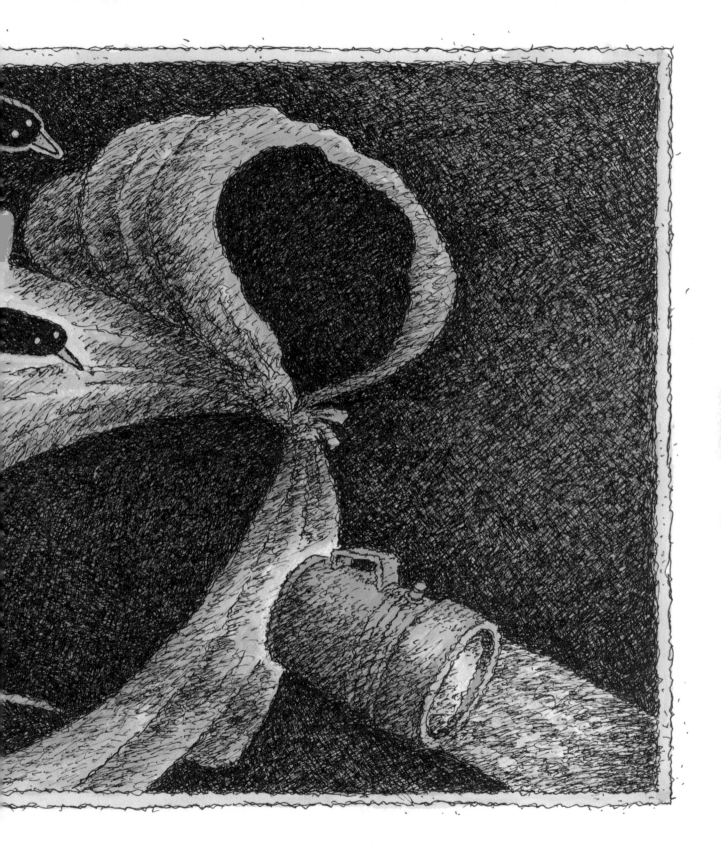

She swallowed the cloak to cover the flashlight.

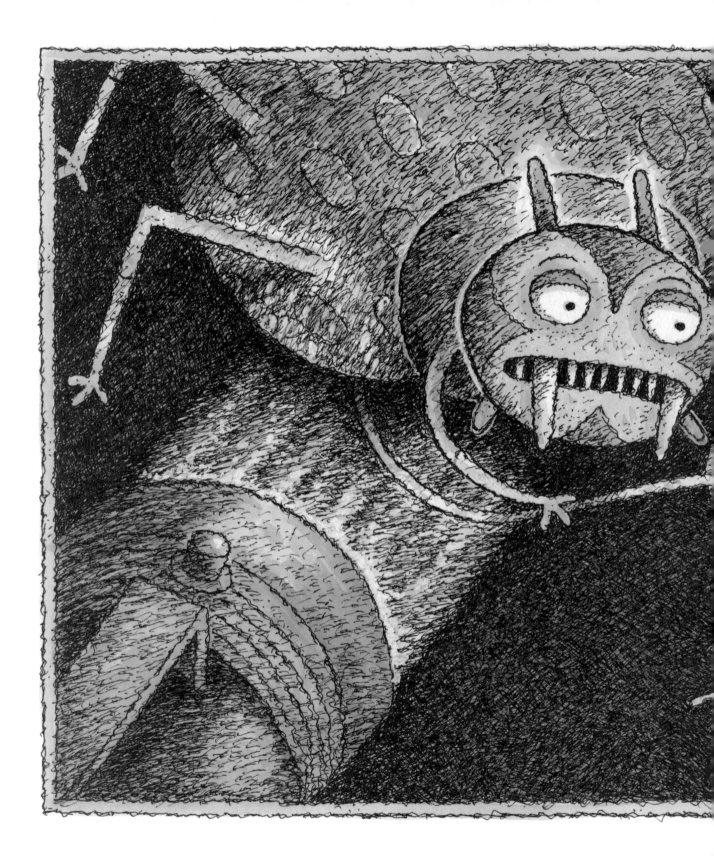

She swallowed the flashlight to brighten the spider.

She swallowed the spider to string up the mask.

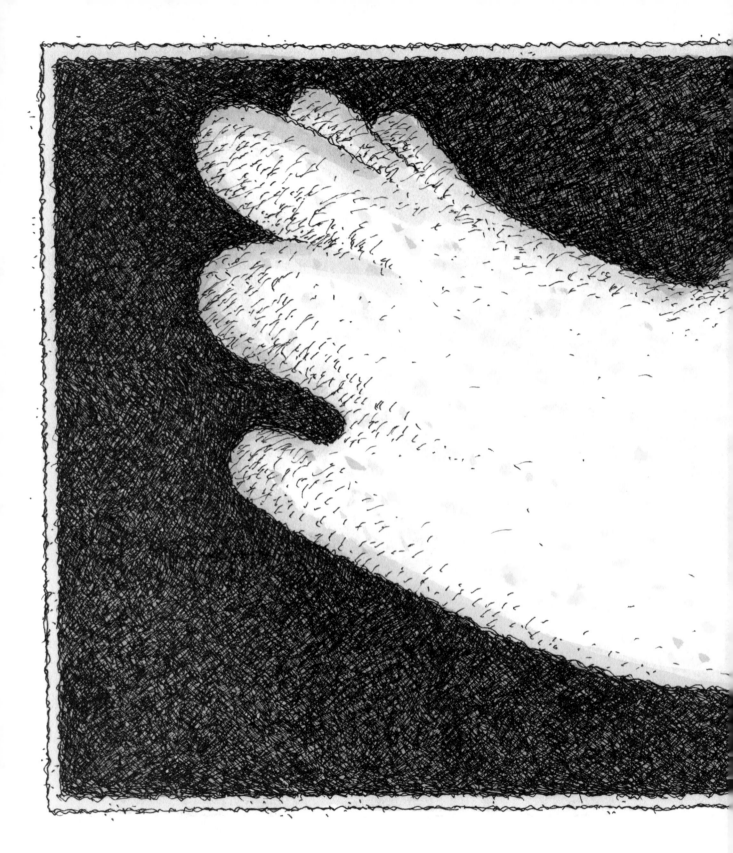

She swallowed the mask to hide the ghost.

I don't know why she swallowed a ghost.
But she didn't boast.

There was an old lady who swallowed a potion.
Her plan was set in motion when she swallowed
that potion.

She started to creep as quiet
as a mouse,

to scare all of her friends at the haunted house!

Happy Halloween!